About the Author

Nikke Hawksley lives in Milton in Cambridge and, through walking her dog Stevie, finds out about all the animals she draws and writes about.

Deez

Pet Rapport

ILLUSTRATED HUMOROUS AND TRUE TALES OF PET CHARACTERS

Tiller

Jethro

Bertie

True Stories Hand Illustrated

Illustrated and Written By

Nikke Hawksley

AUSTIN MACAULEY PUBLISHERS™
LONDON • CAMBRIDGE • NEW YORK • SHARJAH

Copyright © Nikke Hawksley 2023

The right of **Nikke Hawksley** to be identified as author and illustrator of this work has been asserted by them in accordance with sections 77 and 78 of the Copyright, Designs and Patents Act 1988.

All rights reserved. No part of this publication may be reproduced, stored in a retrieval system, or transmitted in any form or by any means, electronic, mechanical, photocopying, recording, or otherwise, without the prior permission of the publishers.

Any person who commits any unauthorised act in relation to this publication may be liable to criminal prosecution and civil claims for damages.

This is a work of fiction. Names, characters, businesses, places, events, locales, and incidents are either the products of the author's imagination or used in a fictitious manner. Any resemblance to actual persons, living or dead, or actual events is purely coincidental.

A CIP catalogue record for this title is available from the British Library.

ISBN 9781398491991 (Paperback)
ISBN 9781035848461 (Hardback)
ISBN 9781398492004 (ePub e-book)

www.austinmacauley.com

First Published 2023
Austin Macauley Publishers Ltd®
1 Canada Square
Canary Wharf
London
E14 5AA

For my sister, Francesca McLaren, a talented singer and poet.

Baxter

Many thanks to the pet owners who kindly supplied me with the material for this book and supplied me with photographs to draw from for this book. There are six fictional examples - I wonder if you can spot which ones they are. A special thanks to Jane Mynott for her helpful editing.

Table of Content

Molly and Dolly	10
Simba Archbold	12
Lenny Jenner	14
Tara Freeman	16
Bertie Knibbs	18
Dylan Hullis	20
Tommy Needing	22
Dash Harradine	24
Olive King	26
Casper Richardson	28
Bailey Wood's Coldplay Vigil	30
Merlot Harvey	32
Sam & Suzy Price	34
Lady Jenner's Call	36
Oakley Cesaro	38
Minnie Bliss	40
Rafferty Mynott	42
Vinnie Ayms Awake	44
Vinnie Asleep	46
Snowflake Bagley	48
Charlie Taylor	50

Buster Ledingham	52
Billy Cox	54
Google Bosworth	56
Alfie Herring	58
Tiller and Truffle	60
Arturius James Baker	62
Gigi Steele	64
Copper Sivier	66
Jethro Hawksley's Diary	68
Apatchy McCormick	70
Angel Green	72
Jack Hawksley	74
Socks Booth	76
Cassy McKenzie	78
Cooky Collison	80
Felis Catus	82
Gemma Addy	84
Bubba Scarfe	86
Geoffrey Scarfe	88
Zoey Corkin	90
Stevie Hawksley	92
Teleporting Cuddles	94
Oscar Nichols	96

Molly and Dolly

Dolly's a staffie named after a singer
Molly's just Molly, but she's a dead ringer
It really is useful that both their names rhyme
If either is called – they arrive the same time

They grin 'til they gleam
And have a huge smiley mouth
They're a dental dream team
Teeth displayed North and South

They make you smile too
Their grins are so huge
You can never be blue
Why, you'd have to be Scrooge

Their patent good mood
Makes a hyper wide grin
So, besides all their food
The bowl would fit in

So, here's to pooch pals
Please stay so beguiling
You're such lovely gals
You keep us all smiling

Molly Hurrell & Dolly Lawrence

Simba Archbold

Naughty Simba Archbold,
Houdini Labrador
He's there and then he isn't
It's done with Sleight of Paw

Was the gate left open?
Or really, was it closed?
Was the latch just faulty?
Or was it Simba-nosed?

Don't leave your food residing
Don't leave things in good faith
He isn't law-abiding
Why, he could crack a safe

And as for stopping exits
With safety fool-proof fence
He'll climb just like a monkey
These Humans are just dense!

So set some sturdy shiplap
Or build another wall
Simba Houdini Archbold
Will overcome them all

Simba Archbold

Lenny Jenner

I heard you bought a "gift" for Keith
And forced it through the door
Poor Heather had to grit her teeth
And almost trapped your paw

Now it seems your leg is hurt
And everyone's upset
Clumsy boy, be more alert
Don't make poor Heather fret

Your photo softly sleeping
Wrapped up so nice and warm
Shows loving eyes are keeping
A watch to stop more harm

So, Lenny keep on healing
But take your time and rest
You look cute and appealing
And keeping safe is best

Lenny Jenner

Tara Freeman

A little snub nose and brown liquid eyes
She looks so very appealing
She's a super soft babe, with a little surprise
Wherever she goes, she's scene stealing

First that tiny snub nose will wrinkle and twist
Then little pearl teeth will appear
At first you might think that it's something you missed
Until the low growling you hear

It's only because when you're cute, people choose
To constantly try cuddling and petting
And sometimes this Diva just wants to snooze
And growling is all you'll be getting

But Davina, her Mum, understands her just so
And Tara's happy to be in her arms
And as long as her Mum just doesn't let go,
From a distance, please admire her charms

So small little girl, we see your reserve
You're the Rock that your Mum loves so much
We will give the respect you so richly deserve
And remember to "Look, But Don't Touch"

Tara Freeman

Bertie Knibbs

I know I once was a stray feral,
And so scarily, terribly, wild
That I put any stranger in peril
But now I'm so gentle and mild

You make me purr
Off the Richter scale
You stroke my soft fur
And play with my tail

I feel safe and get slack
Now you are my Mum
I don't want to go back
To being a bum

Make me purr yet again
And no more will I roam
My gentle refrain
Is an anthem to Home

Bertie Knibbs

Dylan Hullis

Clever Dylan Hullis
Canine Author Without Bite
Such an earnest little face
Is both focused and polite

He has his Listening Ears
On duty all the time
There're no confusion fears
He understands real fine

His latest dissertation
(I think you get the vibe)
Elevates his station
As Canine Master Scribe

Its title "Paws for Thought"
Is for Christmas time release
It is most finely wrought
And outlined for World Peace

So, when his eyes seek yours
And enquiry sits therein
You know his thoughtful brain
And sweet nature lies within

Dylan Hullis

Tommy Needing

Tommy Whippet Needing
Was in a sorry state
All his friends were streamlined
But he was overweight

His owner Patsy Needing
(Who Tommy thought was Mum)
Thought by over feeding
She was kinder to his tum

She was fond of saying
"How Tommy loves his food"!
But he couldn't join in playing
And others thought him rude

One day he tried some chasing
Like when he was a pup
But fell down backward facing
And couldn't get back up

"I'll have to take him walkie"
Thought Patsy, "to a vet"
The vet said "Gosh, he's porky"!
"At least four stone, I bet".

Now Tommy's on a diet
To get a micro waist
He's kept it very quiet
But already he's been chased

And he didn't topple over
Or couldn't get back up
He's really back in clover
Like when he was a pup

So, Patsy knows of feeding
What she didn't know before
Give him what he's "Needing"
And not a morsel more

Tommy Needing

Before

After

Dash Harradine

Mirror, Mirror, on the wall
Why did God make Dash so small?
He's undisputed "Dog in Charge"
His courage? Bigger than a barge!

How can a tiny little mite
Not be afraid of large dogs' bite?
Yet he will bark and "tell them off"
And they will bow, or scarper off

For his authority and gait
Underpins the Nanny State
Of Uber Pooch and El Supreme
No one can best Dash Harradine

Mirror, Mirror, on the Wall
Prove his outfits "on the ball"
Red Hoodie modelled a La Dash
Is worn with flair and such panache

So, Little Man, how can you be
So large a personality?
You're proof a canine mini-moke
Does not denote faint hearted folk

Dash Harradine

Olive King

I was out with a friend, we were running
When he tied me up outside a shop
Someone thoughtless, nasty, and cunning
Grabbed my lead, someone I couldn't stop

I had only known kindness and trust
And I loved my real owners to bits
So when this man did what he must
I didn't know how to resist

I was taken to darkness and strangeness
I longed for my Dad and my Mum
I was lonely and filled with a sadness
Wondering when my salvation would come

I didn't know Twitter and Facebook
Were full of my plight nationwide
Hundreds were trying to help and to look
Where a stolen pup might still survive

I was seen three hundred miles away
And though it couldn't possibly be
My owner came out straight away
On the chance that it really was me

And though I can't talk or say "Thank you"
My heart, it was filled to the brim

When I saw him, my paws nearly flew
I was glad that it really was him.

So, kind people out there who helped find me
Please know I'm no longer alone
For your efforts and kindness did help me
And there really is no place like Home

Olive King

Casper Richardson

Casper does the Collie Crouch
He's an expert in the field
One minute he is standing up
But please keep your eyes peeled

In the long grass, you can't see him
He disappears real quick
Lying flat out on his tummy
It is his favourite trick

He's able to observe which dog
He then needs to round up
He'll keep his "pack" together
Whether human child or pup

He's very good at running,
He's affectionate and sweet
His recall's simply stunning
His posture crisp and neat

So, Casper, heed your training
You're certainly no slouch
It's very entertaining
When you do the Collie Crouch

Casper Richardson

Bailey Wood's Coldplay Vigil

Where have they gone?
I'll wait by the door
I'll wait 'til I'm old
I'll just sit on the floor

I don't understand
Why they are not here
"Gone to see a band"
Means a long time, I fear

I won't touch my plate
Even when they cajole
Not till morning's here, mate
Will I eat from my bowl

Not till Peter applies
My A.M. cuddle and pet
So I know it's not lies
And I don't need to fret

When dawn shows, as it must
And proves daylight has come
Then I'll eat till I bust
Cos I'm with Dad and Mum

Bailey Wood

Merlot Harvey

Merlot Harvey's cunning plot
(He likes to be up higher)
Is to commandeer his special spot
Atop the washer dryer

In a basket blue and plastic
(It's a human laundry drop)
He thinks that it's fantastic
And it is his favourite stop

It lets him watch his mum
And the angle is just so
The position is quite plum
And he cannot let it go

Don't ask him please to move
While you try and wash your stuff
He'll strongly disapprove
And all you'll get is "Wuff"

So Merlot Harvey stay
And watch your lovely mum
And later when you play
She'll do the laundry run

Merlot Harvey

Sam & Suzy Price

Sam can watch the TV – a very special feat
(Most dogs can't see things flat)
He'll bark away at Corrie Street
Because it has a cat

Suzy's fur is made of curls
Each has a coloured ball
Blue for boys and red for girls
They've excellent recall

Suzy doesn't know an infant
Can't throw her coloured ball
She's by prams in an instant
To drop her playful call

Sam and Suzy navigate
Who needs an A to Zed?
Somehow, they always gravitate
To any mobile bed

They love each other dearly
And move with one accord
Both gentle and more clearly
A loving home's reward

Sam & Suzy

Lady Jenner's Call

Hey, Milo, let's go down the pond
The one at the end of the garden
Let's go now, I know you're fond
Of frog watching – beg your pardon?

Oh no, don't worry 'bout getting green
And muddy from the goo
Heather's keen to keep us clean
And she'll know what to do

You back me up and I'll dunk my nose
In algae green and thick
Those frogs live under there, I s' pose
And move about real quick

I'm the one that leads the pack
And delivers "gifts" galore
That Keith will find around the back
Yes, ten's the latest score!

So watch my back, while I respond
To jumping frogs at play
Hey, Milo let's go down the pond
Those cheeky frogs will pay!

Lady

Milo

Oakley Cesaro

Oakley, Oh Oakley – what have you done?
My post was important
And now there is none

I'll never know if I inherited cash
From an old distant rellie
Or was owed a huge stash
From a quiz on the telly

The remains of my letters
Festoon the stairwell
My elders and betters
Now cannot tell

If I love them or not
Since I can't read their script
All is mullered and shredded
And SO Oakley nipped

Oakley Cesaro, though I love you my boy
I think I might find you a better employ

I heard that a company dealing with waste
Needs helpers who have a particular taste
For paper and documents, so tasty to chew
Oakley, oh Oakley – would THAT occupy you?

Oakley Cesaro

Minnie Bliss

She has to watch her figure
As she knows the word for "treat"
So her tummy's getting bigger
And much nearer to her feet

Affectionate and feisty
But in a well-meant way
Though London trips are pricey
She'd go there every day

If you take her to a pub
She needs a ringside seat
So she's at the central hub
And part of the elite

Sun worshipper, go-getter
She loves that duvet down
The more sun shines the better
And rain gets her "paws down"

Minnie has such joie de vivre
And thinks her mum's so cool
Rachelle loves her Minnie Diva
For her it's "Dachshunds Rule"

Minnie & Rachelle Bliss

Rafferty Mynott

Rafferty Mynott – little speed freak
Gallops so fast – all you see is a streak

Ears pinned back by the force
Of his flight, having fun
As he follows the course
Of a hare on the run

His tail, which ends in a cute semi curl
Has a sweet tassel finish
The colour of pearl

He's an avid explorer, with amazing finesse
He can return within seconds without GPS

Jaunty and springy, he's a svelte little gent
With his pals he'll play-fight
Till his energy's spent
Though he has, so it seems, an unending supply
While others relax, he goes speeding by

So, Rafferty Mynott – we look on with awe
At your charisma and charm
We are held in your paw

Rafferty Mynott

Vinnie Ayms Awake

When Training Takes Forever

Please don't get discouraged
Or feel you must give up
He really will be worth it
He's such a lovely pup

He doesn't know he's naughty
But because you love him so
It's sadly unrewarding
And seems too far to go

If he knew his bad behaviour
Caused his owner so much grief
That a tear escaped this morning
And stole Hope like a thief

He'd be a Model Beagle
He'd never, ever, stray
He'd Sit and Stay and Leave It
On order every day

So, understand that Vinnie
Though playing, still, he hears
He really didn't mean to
Cause those unhappy tears

Vinnie Ayms Awake

Vinnie Asleep

A Brief Pause in Activity

Sometimes a Whirlwind pauses
In its electric flight
Sometimes a silence causes
Smiles of wonder and delight

Sometimes a cracker halts
And fizzles out too soon
Or even lightning bolts
Can cease their sonic boom

Sometimes young Vinnie Ayms
Just has to lay him down
And forfeit all his claims
To Top Dog and Best Clown

Sometimes there is a silence
Which is taken to extremes
As with gentle snoring cadence
Vinnie dreams his Vinnie dreams

Vinnie Asleep

Snowflake Bagley

Joni Bagley left a crate
To get some tape to use
So didn't see her cat Snowflake
Creep inside for a snooze

The box was quickly taped up tight
With Snowflake warm inside
And left all cosy overnight
Until the morning ride

Snowflake made no single sound
When she was weighed for post
Not even when stamped "Worthing-bound"
And heading for the coast

For eight whole days poor Snowflake went
Without a single drink
From Cornwall she was being sent
That's further than you think

Meanwhile Joni looked everywhere
And missed her Snowflake's ways
She pasted posters, tore her hair
And cried for seven days

Snowflake was up in Worthing now
And the parcel had arrived

They thought they heard a faint miaow
Yes, Snowflake had survived!

Poor Snowflake was so weak and yet
Miaows can't be ignored
They kindly took her to a vet
So she could be restored

Soon Joni got a welcome call
And drove down, Worthing bound
Then Snowflake stopped her caterwaul
And she's now safe and sound

Snowflake Bagley

Charlie Taylor

Charlie checks his pee mail
Before he takes a Wee
They line his daily route
With info that is free

They tell him who is ill
They tell him who is out
All sorts of doggie blogs
Flow through his trusty snout

They tell him if they're friendly
Or if they're nasty types
He smells the latest news
In streaming gigabytes

His nose is so efficient
At finding all the news
That if his sight's deficient
There's still plenty to peruse

So, Charlie being old now
Relies on Smelly Vision
To make up for his lack
Of visual recognition

So, keep up all the doggie blogs
Witness Charlie's wagging tail
He cannot see the other dogs
But each pee tells a tale

Charlie Taylor

Buster Ledingham

Buster loves Cakey
A pretend piece of cake
He plays with it daily
All the time he's awake

He knows where it is
Any time of the day
"Where's your friend Cakey"?
Is all Livvy need say

And Buster will find it
And cradle his paws
Around his felt friend
Whom he really adores

He will suck on his "cake"
And won't let it go
It's better than steak
And he cuddles it so

When at last he starts snoozing
Still his vigil he keeps
He carries on schmoozing
Right up till he sleeps

Buster loves Cakey
And he is no fool
Other toys are just flaky
Only Cakey is cool

Buster Ledingham

Billy Cox

I don't know Billy
But I can see
That Billy is his own man

Something there in his eyes
Is making me see
That Billy is his own man

I know he's a cat
And cats always choose
Just who they decide to trust

But Billy's a cat
(And this might be news)
Who only loves those who he must

That magical person is Francine
She has the required cachet

And Billy's a cat
Who is his own man
Which is really all someone can say

Billy Cox

Google Bosworth

I was last in the line when Cherry and John
Decided to give me a home
They wanted to right such a terrible wrong
And were sad to see me alone

Many weeks went past, and I was treated so well
Scars inside and out were still mending
When they let me off lead, I was free for a spell
The beach just seemed never ending

As I ran and I ran I remembered their voices
And how they had treated me kindly
We all live our lives and all make our choices
I slowed and I stopped running blindly

I stopped and I turned, to see where they were
I panicked and ran all the way
But they had both waited and they were still there
In their hearts they had hoped I would stay

I squeezed in between them, like a coat that is lined
And I stayed there, wedged as tight as can be
I finally knew that some humans are kind
And came to love them, as they had loved me.

Google Bosworth

Alfie Herring

Alfie Herring, Soccer Star
The Dog Who Has the Ball
His nose is famous, near and far
This pooch just has it all

His dribbling is no canine drool
(Like some dogs that abound)
And every paw move is so cool
He's such a canny hound

He barks till someone else joins in
His crafty slow roll game
His nifty paw work then cuts in
And puts all else to shame

Another goal has hit the net
I guess it could be worse
But you just ain't seen nothing yet
He even does reverse!

His nose it gets so pink and warm
From nudging, pushing ball
For which his "mum" applies a balm
He really gives his all

He has a special fur lined cage
He's pampered and elite

His jackets – they are all the rage
Why Rooney can't compete

Dear Alfie Herring Super Star
Keep practicing off lead
We know you are the best by far
At least, Pooch Premier League

Alfie Herring

Tiller and Truffle

Tiller gets muddy and covered in burrs
Chasing pheasants as long as she can
Truffle is loyal and thinks Sandra is hers
So, trots behind her, as part of her clan

They curl up together and dream of their walks
Remembering days on their old narrow boat
If they could speak, they'd both give us talks
Of adventures whiles travelling afloat

Such wonderful girls are from the same gene
Truffle pulls her blanket along, like it's glued
She licks her sister, so that she is kept clean,
And ensures all the dirt is removed

They're happy and have such a wonderful time
Between boating and racing off lead
So sweet and good natured, these girls are sublime
And Sandra gives them the love that they need

Tiller and Truffle

Arturius James Baker

He came from a fair so tiny and cute
"Arturius James" seemed the name that would suit

First timid and shy, then increasingly bold
Arturius James was cuddly to hold

He fell in the pond while trying to play
At first no-one saw him when paddling away
Mrs Baker looked up and saw his sad plight
Then rushed out to save him, the poor little mite
Arturius James was full of dismay
And will not touch water, to this very day

He will hop on your lap
While you're watching TV
Or snuggle up close
While you're drinking your tea

He'll scratch to come in if it's wet or it's cold
And lie on his back in the warm fluffy fold
Of a fleece, while he's tickled right under his chin
If a rabbit can smile, why, that's Arthur Jim
Arturius James is a name so noble and fine

Arturius James – Oh Bunny Divine

Arturius James Baker

Gigi Steele

Beautiful Gigi, soulful and sweet
Head cocked to the side
While she waits for her treat

She snorts up a scent
Noisy hovering sound
Up to heaven she's sent
Then returns to the ground

Give her a call, her ears go forward a while
Or blissful in sleep, she will literally smile

Like a racehorse, her gait
While she runs like the wind
An affectionate mate
A true loyal friend

Beautiful Gigi, soulful and sweet
Mild of eye, kind of heart
Makes life so complete

Gigi Steele

Copper Sivier

He grins and he bares all his teeth
Which is weird and a little bit scary,
But he's actually friendly, beneath
He's a Catalan Sheep dog – he's Hairy!

Special friends get his patented smile
At others he will look with disdain
It's his very own special Copp style
Of greeting, as they do when in Spain

A battalion of white teeth will present
In a hairy and fluffy physog
Then a bark underpins his intent
To welcome a la Spanish dog

His bark is a true source of wonder
In water, it just cannot stall
And once his snout is right under
Muffled bubbles still echo his call

So Copper, please bark and faux grin
And do keep having a ball
We know which mood you are in
And it just isn't threatening at all

Copper Sivier

Jethro Hawksley's Diary

I am liking the boarding school my mum sent me to, it seems pretty cool. I feel I am growing bigger by the second but sadly suffered with teething last night. My new mum says it is only a Nylabone that stands between her and Certain Death. I am hoping if I go out today, I might repeat my AMAZING feat of pooing in the earth of the next-door neighbour's front garden. For some reason this boring and fundamental act elicited lots of high-pitched noises from my Mum. I hope she is okay. What else? Oh yes, I met two kind ladies, but they were very scary to look at. I am sorry for you humans with your abnormally long noses – small wonder I am not really at ease when faced with these bizarre proboscises. But you mean well. Had a bit of a restless night – I think it was all this football business as Dad was yelling in the kitchen and Mum didn't let me on the bed in case she squashed me. In the end it was the old routine – I drop off on her chest and she plonks me back in my bed. I had a really good appetite today and slept a lot more which mum said was a good sign I was relaxing and concentrating on growing into a Big Boy. Met Zoey the Pug's grandma whilst sitting on the dividing wall while mum held me steady. She says I am a Good Boy, and my big paws mean I may grow quite large. Roll on the steak dinners ha-ha. PS I still find the coir mat posher than my poo box but Mum says she doesn't mind as it is all about eventually deciding the garden is even posher and it is very early days. PPS, I saw a reflection in the cupboard mirror, but whoever that interloper was, I saw him off. Bit of an odd-looking fella but that is not his fault.

For some reason Dad said I looked like "Churchill". Who is he and do I know him? Whatever. Dad does occasionally call me Winston, now, but then I can think of a few things to call him when he trod on me today. He was very sorry and made it up to me by lulling me to sleep singing "Beautiful Dreamer" which I must say did the trick.

I seem to have a Discerning Ear. I felt my head twist every which way when mum asked Alexa (another person I have not met) to play Simon and Garfunkel. They made lovely noises which I approve of. Mum doesn't understand why Amy Winehouse had the opposite effect. I got a bit stressed out and she had to break out the peanut butter bones. Perhaps her mournful tone was not conducive – and what is Tankeray, anyway?

There remains a lot for me to understand about humans, but I am determined to succeed.

To Do List: 1. Join puppy training class so I can meet other rookie pups and people of my own size 2. Tell dad to look where he is going 3. Learn to tell the Alexa person to tune in to Puppy Pop Hour so I can practice my moves ready for when I am a Big Boy and become a Babe Magnet. Scratch the last one I am already a Babe Magnet. P.S. Had my usual Fast and Furious Hour workout this evening in prep for pole axing around the 9pm mark. Dad calls it my "Bomber Harris" routine.

Who ARE these people??

Jethro

Apatchy McCormick

Apatchy didn't understand
Why dogs looked at his tail
It really was quite in demand
– Attractive without fail

He always smiled at a new friend
And looked them in the eye
But still they faced the other end
And often passed him by

One day he asked a passing Pug
The question on his mind
"Why did you give your lead a tug
Then look at my behind"?

"Don't you know"? Answered the pup
"We must check each other's rears"?
"The tale is old, but listen up"
– Apatchy was all ears

"When God first made a dog from dust
He made some loving hearts
Then slowly added Oil of Trust
And fur to all the parts"

"He'd nearly finished, adding feet
Creating Man's Best Friends
But though the job appeared complete,
He forgot about our ends"

"A tail for every single pup
Was waiting to attach
But in their haste to partner up
Some of them didn't match"

"So even now, in modern day,
A strange dog often dares
To check the others style of tail
And see if it is theirs"

Now Apatchy makes quite sure
Whatever glimpse he catches,
The other's tail is quite secure
And mainly – that it matches

Apatchy and Pug

Angel Green

Beautiful Angel – Persian tom cat supreme
He follows his mistress – after all, they're a team

He's terribly handsome, his eyes win the crown
One is green with black edging, the other is brown

He fetches and follows like a loyal canine
And growls at black cats who step out of line

If Kasia has a bath, he'll be there in the sink
If she is out in the sun, he'll turn up in a blink

Now he is old and much slower in ways
But he'll still follow Kasia to the end of his days

Although he is old, he is steadfast and true
Beautiful Angel – here's looking at you.

Angel Green

Jack Hawksley

Jack Hawksley chased rabbits for sport
But he'd never catch them, per se
The reason he always fell short
Was his owner would shoo them away

One day Jack was circling his favourite patch
Near buildings folk work in all day
He sped off like a bullet no-one could catch
His owner still warning his prey

But after 10 minutes with no sign at all
She knew she had cause for concern
It wasn't like Jack not to come to her call
If he could, he would quickly return

Two hours later, completely worn out
She phoned all the offices round
Security guards said they'd give her a shout
The minute the white scamp was found

The day it wore on, but at last news came through
Jack had escaped from a watery demise
A hero had saved him with much derring-do
With the ending a happy surprise

A large moat surrounded an office so deep
That Jack chasing a rabbit, fell in

The sides of it really were terribly steep
So his chance of survival was thin

Meantime Adam thought he'd seen a small pup
Disappear in the water filled moat
For three hours poor Jack had tried to keep up
But exhausted, could not stay afloat

Without hesitation Adam ran out the back
Despite colleagues who stared at him, frowning
He set off alarms, leaping in to save Jack
Who by now, was actually drowning

Kind security guards used hairdryers and coats
To dry Jack, who was cold and distraught
And needless to say, no longer likes moats
And doesn't chase rabbits for sport

Jack Hawksley

Socks Booth

When Catherine saw Socks
She was inside a cage
Rescued by the Blue Cross
Only three years of age

10 kittens she'd had
But they hadn't survived
She was friendly, but sad
Until Catherine arrived

She took her tout suite
And gave her name "Socks"
As she had four white feet
From her toes to her hocks

She had two special beds
A cat flap in the shed
But if a chair was left free
She'd nab that instead

Her fresh water bowl
Was always on hand
But bird water she stole
The taste was less bland

So well done Socks Booth
Your new home was a treat
You were living proof
Cats can land on their feet!

Socks Booth

Cassy McKenzie

At any time, where Lisa goes
Or something's pepper-minted
Cassy follows like a duck
That's nurtured and imprinted

Give up your puzzle board
It's really meant for her
And after re-arranging things
She'll lie on it and purr

You'd think she's keen on minty breath
In fact, it's quite a puzzle
Just how she'll nudge and mew and purr
And give toothpaste a nuzzle

She'll nudge you off your pillow
And doesn't spare your hair
And if she hears John on the phone
She'll act as if he's there

Cassy is her name,
She's a pretty marmalade
And on the bed, her weight
Makes Lisa's legs all splayed

It's clear for all to see
She's found the best of homes
She gets fresh cod, you see
(They confiscate the bones)!

Cassy McKenzie

Cooky Collison

Cooky's age is secret
She's such an acrobat
She acts just like a baby
she's a swedish climbing cat
She flies, jumps and runs
Across the highest roof
If felines have nine lives
Then Cooky is the proof

She loves her Owner Ony
and revels in her charms
She goes everywhere still with her
Just like a babe in arms

So what if she is foreign?
She knows she lives in Britain
At 12 she's really sprightly
And she plays just like a kitten

She may be a furry swede
But she translates every word
Ony knows that this is true
Even though it sounds absurd

When you hold her like a baby
Or stroke her lovely fur
She answers you in English
Which comes out as a purr!

Cooky Collison

Felis Catus

Felis was a clever cat
He knew how to cut hair
He learned it all from Hugo's Gran
And did it with real flair

He knew the latest cuts and trends
His clients loved his paws
He dressed their hair and cut the ends
His work got Facebook scores

His Granny would cut Hugo's hair
But haircuts were so strained
And Felis offered to compare
As Hugo had complained

Felis cut it close and cut it short
Because it was the trend
But Hugo's ears, the scissors caught
He thought it was the end

Enough! He said I want my Gran
She really is the best
And so it was our little man
Found Gran had passed the test

So now he never says a jot
His haircut's such a perk!
Even George will smile a lot
They love their Granny's work!

Felis Catus

Gemma Addy

Little Gemma Addy
Tiny little thing
How does she move about?
Is she pulled by string?

It cannot be with legs
She really gets around
We've never seen her pegs
She's so close to the ground

She moves with flowing motion
Though paw-steps can be heard
Such spooky locomotion
Is both comic and absurd

But though her ghostly limbs
Cause endless fascination
Gemma's tiny pins
Get her to her destination

Gemma Addy

Bubba Scarfe

Bubba Scarfe is worried
It's written on his face
He's wrinkled all his forehead
He knows he's in disgrace

He's chased another bird
Or scared the local cat
He's pounced on something furry
Or made his football flat

Poor Chris is trying to berate him
It is for his own good
But his mournful eyes just make him
Look so misunderstood

He'll whimper if you scold him
And flash his big brown eyes
Until you swear he's crying
It looks as though he tries

He's really just a pup
And full of life and go
It's sad to pull him up
When nature's made him so

So, if Chris does give in
She really can't be blamed
Just one look at him
Makes retribution shamed

Bubba Scarfe

Geoffrey Scarfe

Geoffrey is playing his cello
"Oh, is he a musical cat"?
He's a very affectionate fellow
But doesn't know A from B flat

He stretches his neck so his spine
Adopts an uncomfortable slouch
Then mimics the bent over line
Of a cellist's most musical crouch

His back leg has to wave in the air
He's thorough and self-cleaning
He perks and spruces his hair
Until he's all shiny and gleaming

He hasn't a musical ear
(Though purring is tuneful to Man)
But by bending right over, it's clear
He's keeping his fur spick and span

So next time that you see cello playing,
While crouched in a way that's quite funny
You can be quite confident saying
Geoffrey'd give them a run for their money!

Geoffrey Scarfe

Zoey Corkin

Zoey's bark is more like a yap
She loves company, food and a treat
She will always find a warm lap
Because she's so small and petite

The yap is due to her size
Which, as mentioned, is tiny and neat
This is odd, because I heard tell
There's no end to how much she can eat

She'll give you her "Free Licks on Tap"
She's such an affectionate girl
Please reserve her your lovely warm lap
And she'll soon be along for her seat

Tracy says her pug is a Diva
As she usually gets her own way
But Zoey is just being Zoey
And she always makes Tracy's day

Zoey Corkin

Stevie Hawksley

Stevie, Stevie Hawksley, the disappearing hound
He's an optical illusion when he fools around
He's nowhere to be seen, although he was just there
And now he's really gone - disappeared into thin air

Survey the horizon – do you see a faint spot?
It may be young Stevie, though probably not
He's raced off to nowhere, and where he was seen
Is nothing but space, heaven knows where he's been

I've called and I've called but still there's no sign,
And more often than not, he appears from behind
Just when I think I must call the Police
There he is calm and happy, the curious beast.

I will take him tomorrow, to world famous Crufts,
Which Specialist Category? Why, Teleporting Mutts!
I swear he'll perform on that special day
All I must do is just turn away

He'll soon disappear and when I look back
He'll appear by my side if I just give him slack
He'll win an award – how can I be sure?
His breed has a feature, for which there's no cure
Forget all your Recalls, for those In the Know
He's a Master of Teleporting, the Best in Show

Stevie Hawksley

Teleporting Cuddles

Stevie's gone all weird
I wish I knew how
He's just disappeared
From the here and now

There he was, just evading
Young Florence and Freddy
Then he starts fading
Going weird and cob-webby!

He'll come back, be assured
There will be a reprieve
He just got bored
And decided to leave

Ah, here he is now
Behind that big hedge
Don't look at him, please
That will give him the edge

He'll fade into your arms
Like he was there all the time
To submit to your charms
In a cuddle sublime

Teleporting Cuddles

Oscar Nichols

Oscar has a stick store
At the entrance to the park
A handy cache that comes to paw
Even when it's dark

His mum is Margaret, his dad is Dick
They know he's fussy with his stick
It just makes sense
He takes his pick
From Oscar's Stick Store

The sticks are more like logs
Too big for many dogs
But Oscar, he can fill his clogs
From Oscar's Stick Store

Oscar Nichols

Pet Rapport is a collection of true pet stories, humorous and original. They are illustrated by the author from photos taken by their owners.

Milton Keynes UK
Ingram Content Group UK Ltd.
UKHW022032181123
432826UK00005B/76